To Jane

Copyright © 1991 by Daniel Lehan

All rights reserved.

Library of Congress Cataloging in Publication Data
CIP Data is available.

First published in the United States 1992 by
Dutton Children's Books
a division of Penguin Books USA Inc.

Published simultaneously in Canada by
Fitzhenry & Whiteside Limited, Toronto
Originally published in Great Britain in 1991 by ABC, All Books for Children,
a division of the All Children's Company Ltd
33 Museum Street, London WC1A 1LD

First American Edition   Printed in Hong Kong
10 9 8 7 6 5 4 3 2 1
ISBN 0-525-44878-0

This is not a book about dodos

DANIEL LEHAN

Dutton Children's Books

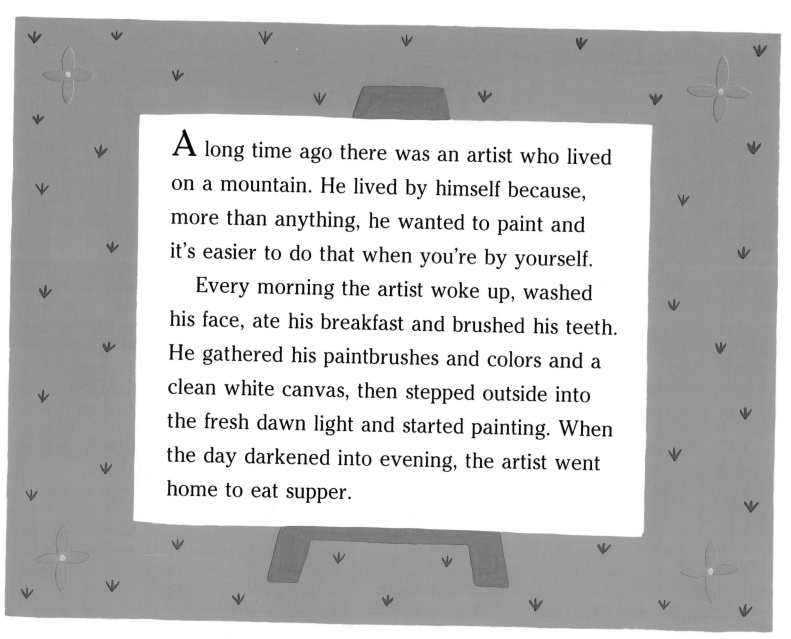

A long time ago there was an artist who lived on a mountain. He lived by himself because, more than anything, he wanted to paint and it's easier to do that when you're by yourself.

Every morning the artist woke up, washed his face, ate his breakfast and brushed his teeth. He gathered his paintbrushes and colors and a clean white canvas, then stepped outside into the fresh dawn light and started painting. When the day darkened into evening, the artist went home to eat supper.

One morning the artist awoke as usual, washed and ate as usual and brushed his teeth as usual. But when he opened his door, *nothing* was usual. Sitting on his mountain was a huge flock of dodos.

The artist
blinked twice
and rubbed his eyes.

Now, maybe you don't know what a dodo looks like, or perhaps you think you know, but you aren't absolutely, positively sure. Well, I'll tell you about them. A distant ancestor of mine actually saw a live dodo. I wish I could say he encountered this dodo in an exotic land, but he didn't. In truth he saw the bird in a cage at a village fair.

Above the cage was a sign that said A Bewildering and Unique Specimen of Nature, Captured at Enormous Expense and Risk, from the Very Farthest and Smallest Corner of the World. After seeing this dodo, my ancestor felt compelled to write the following poem:

Ode to a Dodo

Of all strange creatures here in sight,

It's of the dodo I'll now write.

A clumsy bird that, my, oh, my,

Has such small wings, it cannot fly;

And legs so stubby, stout, and small

It's wondrous that it moves at all!

It croaks out ugly, wheezing cries,

And, in between its bright pink eyes,

A twisted bill makes Dodo scowl—

It is a most uncommon fowl!

So, you can see that the dodo has an odd appearance.

Faced with so many of these bizarre birds, the artist was deeply troubled. He didn't see how he could continue to paint landscapes when the mountain was covered with dodos.

"I'll have to make them leave," he thought. He yelled as loudly as he could and ran about, waving his arms.

The dodos looked at him and then at one another. The artist was sure he even heard one laugh. But they did not leave.

The artist decided to ignore the birds and carry on as if they had never wandered onto the mountain.

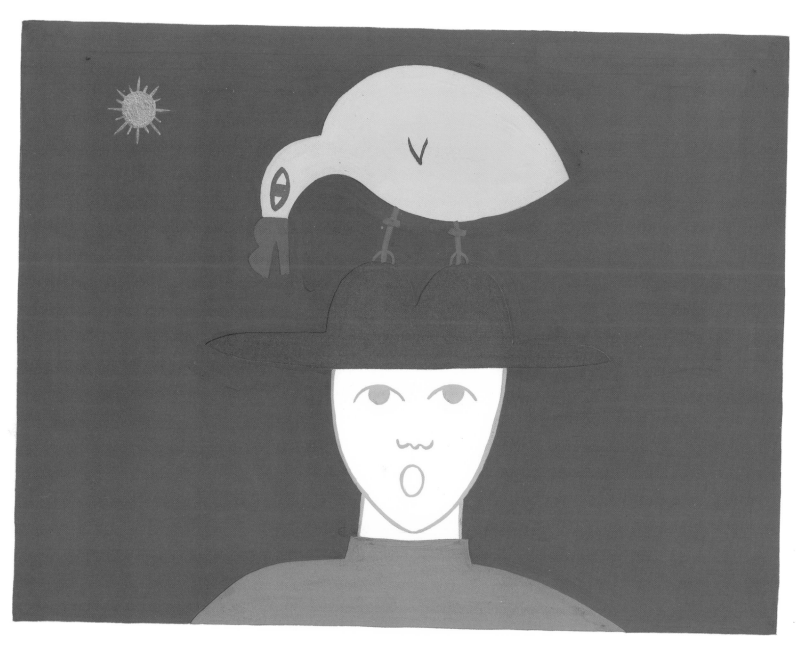

It's difficult to ignore one dodo,

but it's impossible to ignore a whole flock of them.

The artist noticed that some shapes in his
magnificent landscapes bore a strong resemblance
to dodos. The more he pretended they weren't there,
the more they seemed to appear in his pictures.

The artist thought. He could leave his mountain and find another one. But he didn't want to leave his mountain, and the dodos might follow him anyway.

There was only one thing to do: paint the dodos!
Once he had decided, the artist began painting
immediately. He soon found out that it is as impossible
to paint dodos as it is to ignore them.

They kept moving around. First one moved a leg,
then another stretched its wings. Sometimes they
struck wild, flamboyant poses. And the artist
kept having to start again.

But, after a while,
he found that the dodos
had a charm of their
own, and he began
to enjoy painting them.

Every morning the dodos woke the artist with a loud dodo chorus. He washed his face, ate his breakfast, brushed his teeth, and went outside to paint.

Every time he finished a picture, he hung it up on his wall. Through blistering summers and nose-nipping winters, the artist painted pictures of dodos—young, old, and in between.

He felt part of
the dodos' lives.

One morning, the artist woke up later than usual. There had been no dodo chorus. After washing and eating and brushing he went outside to paint.

There were no dodos.

At first, he thought they were playing hide-and-seek,

but he searched the whole mountain

and all he could find
were some old nests and
a few tattered feathers.

The artist went home and waited for the dodos,
but they didn't come back that day, or the next,
or the day after.

He remembered how he had wanted the dodos
to leave when they first appeared. Now he wished
they would come back. He missed them.

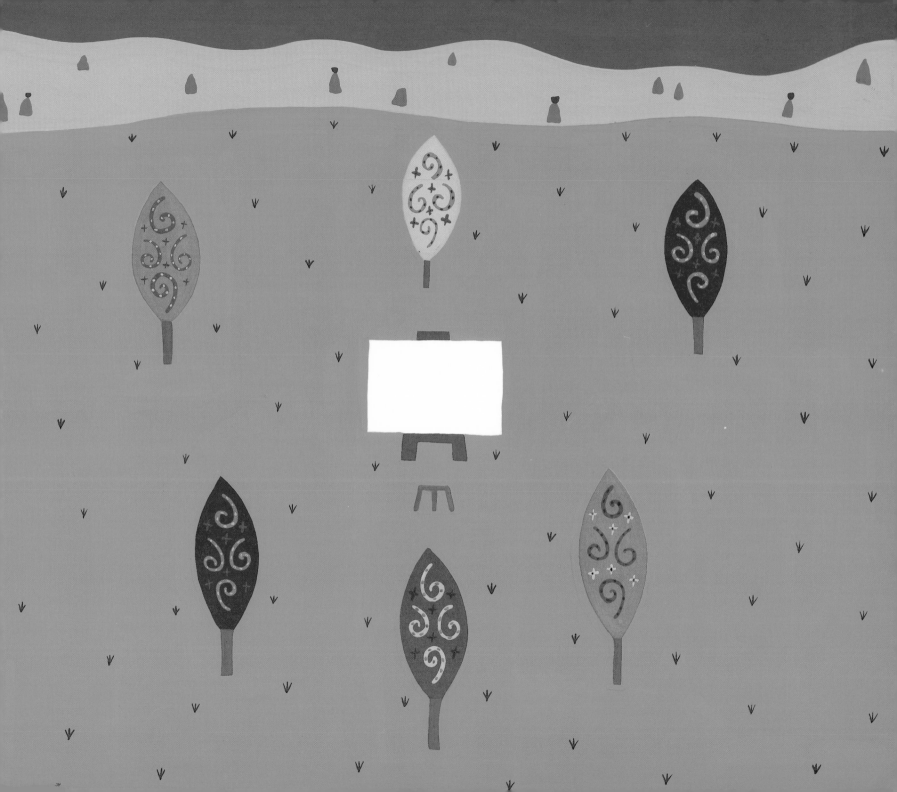

The artist realized what he had to do. He took down all the pictures he had ever painted of the dodos and put each one on the mountain, facing his home.

And then he sat down to paint.